Muscle and

Louise Finnigan

First published June 2021 by Fly on the Wall Press
Published in the UK by Fly on the Wall Press
56 High Lea Rd
New Mills
Derbyshire
SK22 3DP

www.flyonthewallpress.co.uk
Copyright Louise Finnigan © 2021
ISBN: 9781913211448

To Sarah,
And to all those who wander in and out
Of different worlds,
Without losing their feet.

It's lunchtime and there's only me and Mrs Muldowney in the room. She reads my coursework and I sit hunched in my coat looking at the display on the wall behind her. It's all linguistics. Keywords typed black on white, then glued onto faded peach sugar paper. Some of the definitions are starting to curl at the edges and peel away. The colour underneath is brighter.

Through the window cold clouds pass quickly by, but Mrs Muldowney remains unmoving and unmoved. I want to catch her nodding or twitching her mouth the way she does if she's amused or exasperated or pissed off. *Paralinguistic features*, she calls them. But she isn't using any, so I have no clue if the piece is going to get the grade it needs.

The path to Durham is all hard edges and humourless demands. Straight As in History, Politics and English Language. A string pulled taut, with no give. *I'm* meant to give and give and give but I cannot presume anything, that's what I've been told. There are a few lines about personal circumstances on my statement, but I can't be too reliant on that. I must prove myself. I must write until my shoulder muscles ache with all-night essays.

I sigh and the sound is lost in the rasp of paper as Mrs Muldowney turns the page. There is no flicker of thought or emotion on her face, only the flexing of an ankle beneath the desk; her patent leather toe rotating in slow, concentrated circles.

Back when the task was set, it seemed easy. Record people speaking and write an essay about it. Apply linguistic

7

concepts, link to research or theory or whatever.

"But it should be *more* than that," Mrs Muldowney told us. "The best investigations will *raise* questions as well as answering them. They will reflect something that matters to you, something personal." I pulled a face at the smoothness of my desk as she spoke. As if 'personal' is what those posh old twats at the exam board really want. "The best pieces will give something," she said, "that speaks about the world *you're* from."

I give it to her now. I feel the giving. The something, the thing that is mine, slipping away as she reads.

*

This investigation will record, transcribe, and analyse the language of young men talking about their hometown and the extent to which they want to leave it. The speakers are long- term inhabitants of one of Manchester's most deprived housing estates, notorious for high levels of crime and low levels of employment. The analysis will focus on the presence (or absence) of features typically associated with layers of society which might be described as 'the underclass.'

The rain falls misty and soft as I walk down Shadow Brook Road, towards Stephen's. I've got the tape-recorder and some paper in my bag, along with the six bottles of *Hooch* I crammed in before leaving the house.

"Where you off, now?" Mum said, angling her head awkwardly from her place by the telly. I muttered something about college and let the door bang shut. No point trying to explain.

I breathe the drip of browning leaves, the fog of airport fumes and the wafting smells of chip-pan and spliff. There's been a christening at the pub and women wobble across the wet carpark in heels and wave at me, balancing foil trays of leftover sandwiches on their hips. Through the door behind them, disco lights slide from green to red and back again, and smokers slump into the comforting stink of their ashtrays. It's depressing, I suppose. Most people would see it as depressing.

But what they don't see is that this land is rich. And when I say rich, I mean fertile. Dark with energy. I learned about it in primary school when we did local geography. Another project on 'my world', but this one felt good. We looked at old maps and interviewed our nannas and stuff. We found out that the land used to be chopped up into allotments for locals to dig turf for their fires and they were told to re-place the top layer of peat each time so the whole thing would grow again. Ever since, I've imagined it under our feet. Re-fuelling itself over centuries. Humming up against the concrete crusts of its surface. Smouldering under overgrown gardens. Burning quietly beneath the sodden benches of the park. It throbs through us when we shout or laugh or fuck. It makes everything light up brighter than it should.

I stop to fish out a cigarette, then turn onto Willowsway where passing cars slice at puddles and headlights sparkle the rain. The questions I need to ask are troubling me. I'm not sure how to frame them in a way that's fair, without digging a pit for my friends to fall into. For Stephen to fall into.

Typically, in male-to-male interactions we would expect to see examples of competitive behaviour such as interruption, increase in volume and use of expletives to hold the floor and maintain the attention of the listener. In interactions between men of this socioeconomic class, research suggests such features will be even more prominent with behaviour driven by aggression and desire for dominance.

When I asked Stephen about the transcript, he squinted into his pint then nodded, as if it was the kind of thing he did all the time.

"Alright. If it's for college an' that. Just don't make me look daft that's all."

"Don't make *yourself* look daft," I said and poked him on the chest. Just lightly, under his collarbone, to show I was joking. And he put his drink down and looked at the spot where my fingers had grazed his shirt.

I've only been to his new flat once before. Up a little alley behind the off-licence and the boarded-up laundrette. It's one of those that used to be a three-bedroomed family house before getting split in two. Stephen's is upstairs and I can see he's put all the lights on because he probably thinks bright windows make it look cosy. As I get closer, I hear N-Trance blasting out like it was when he first moved in and we sat together on the second-hand sofa he'd managed to lug up the stairs. I haven't looked at the card he gave me since then. I can't stand to see the wobble of his handwriting, the crumpled edges of the envelope where he'd held it in his hands for too long before saying: "I wrote this thing for you." It makes me glad that tonight, Mikey will be there. And Connor too.

The three participants are aged between twenty and twenty-five. Stephen (24) is the occupier of the property and the subject best known to the interviewer. Mikey (25), is Stephen's long-term friend from the local comprehensive and Connor (20) is Stephen's cousin.

I'm trying to remember what Mrs Muldowney said about making sure everyone has a fair chance at participating and how we need to remain neutral even if the conversation takes a turn we weren't expecting. I'm thinking about this, and flicking ash at the kerb, when I see Darren Naylor at the downstairs window.

I had thought the flat under Stephen's was empty. I had thought Naylor was still locked up. But he's right there, shadowed but meaty behind the glass. His eyes stare past me at cracked paving slabs, at bollards smashed into stumps by speeding cars. He shifts into the light and I see how his hands are clasped under his face, with dark-lined knuckles pressed into the scarred stubble of his chin. I feel a grisly need to know what he's dreaming up. The dreams of a dog chained by the ankle. Then his eyes slide up to meet mine. His lips curl and I see the tip of his tongue slip out to wet flashing teeth.

I bash at Stephen's door with my fist until I hear him turning the latch on the other side. He beams at me. He has his best shirt on, and I wish that he didn't.

"Jade's here," he shouts up the stairs. I follow him, turning my face from the smell of his aftershave. In the front room, the music's turned right up and every surface shudders with bass. Connor shifts off the sofa and crouches on the floor under the window. Mikey's at the table sprinkling rolling tobacco into the creased cradle of an extra-long Rizla. Stephen's showing me things he's bought for the flat. There's a plasticky-looking canvas of the New York skyline and a super-sized ashtray that swooshes round when you press a button. There's one orange, satin-effect cushion which he slides towards me with a proud kind of smile as I sit next to him on the sofa. I don't mention Naylor, but the name lingers like rot in my mouth. "It's looking nice in here," I say instead, and Stephen looks round at the place nodding to himself.

At the point of interview, none of the subjects are in full time employment although Stephen is applying to be trained as a joiner and Mikey has some part-time work as a security guard in the local precinct.

"No bottle-opener," shouts Mikey, pointing at the drink I'm taking out of my bag. "Give it here, then." The music is too loud for me to hear the metal cap making that crunching, buckling sound inside his mouth but it's hard not to imagine it. He passes the dripping bottle back and I take a few gulps, looking away from the yellow cave of his teeth as he smiles.

I check the tape, slipping it in and out of the deck. I take out the paper so I can record their actions as well as their words. The whole thing makes me feel almost professional and the thought giggles through me as I take another swig.

Stephen's up on his feet again by the Hi-Fi speakers, picking out the tunes we should line up next and Mikey's leaning forward, asking if the transcript will make him famous.

"My English teacher will have to read it," I tell him with a shrug. "And maybe the exam board." Mikey rubs his hands together and Stephen tells him not to piss about because this will go towards my Uni application. And it's true. It will.

The transcript uses capitalisation to indicate an increase in volume and underlining to show where words have been spoken with emphasis. Every speaker, apart from the interviewer, is identified by their first initial.

I nod at Stephen to show we should probably get started and he turns the music down, just a little.

"Let's crack on then," he says, playing boss. We all move closer and stare down through the tiny window where the cassette wheels wait. I press record and the space around

12

us sharpens with the sense of something listening.

S: It's on (.) she's started it mate

C: Turn the music off

M: Don't turn it off (.) turn it up

Interviewer: I'm gonna ask the questions now (…) right (.) okay (.) so how long've you been living around here then (.) on this estate

S: Well you know *(coughs)* like yourself-

M: 1970 (.) year I was born

S: Like yourself and Mikey here (..) whole time really (.) born and-

M: Born and fuckin' BRED *(laughs)*

Interviewer: Connor?

C: (…) same

M: 'cept you weren't born in 1970 mate (.) coz I'm five years older (.) you're like (.) fuckin' (.) nineteen or summat (..) pass us one of them beers

Interviewer: And how would you describe it (.) around here (..) what kind of place is this

M: What kind of place is it *(laughs)*

Mikey's enjoying it already, I can tell. His eyes keep flicking down to the black-slotted hole soaking up his voice. His face is flushed and his accent's getting thicker. 'Older' becomes 'old-oh', hanging open like a cough. The 'uh' in 'fuck' is wide as a bucket. These are the sounds I will lose, the sounds that are already being squeezed out of me. College

13

has started it and Durham will finish it. I try out a mental picture of myself, walking to a lecture on some crisp autumn morning. Consider my voice, contributing an idea in a seminar. These are tight-lipped places where the words might be longer, but the vowels are measured and clipped. I've learned how to contain the sounds I make when I open my mouth, to cut them back like neatly-trimmed hedges in better areas. To clothe myself in a fitting vocabulary. But I love the way they speak, the way I speak when I'm with them. The way Stephen drawls as he leans, almost affectionately, towards the tape.

S: Nah (…) the place is a shithole (..) but also it's like (..) I'm proud to be from round here and it's about the people innit (.) at the end of the day it's about the people and-

M: 'cept when I was inside-

S: And if you ask me nan (.) this is the best place in the world-

M: 'cept when I was in PRISON (..) six weeks (…) wasn't livin' here THEN was I

S: No (.) no mate you wasn't

Interviewer: Connor (.) what do you think

C: Errr (..) yeah (…) the people are sound

M: Oh aye the people are fuckin' LOVELY yeah *(burps)*

S: Not everyone (.) You get your tossers like-

M: Some mad cunts out there (.) proper mad like

A new song begins, synthetic and swelling, and it occurs to me that we should probably turn the music off. Not just because of the sound quality on the tape. But because of the glint of those eyes from the room underneath, waiting,

14

surely, for some excuse. But Stephen is standing in the middle of the carpet demonstrating his swivel ashtray like a man living a dream. It'd be cruel to wake him. And anyway, he's close enough to the tape for it to absorb him word for word. Mikey's being picked up nice and clear as well, laughing loud and pulling a bag of weed from his top pocket. It's Connor I'm not so sure of. He leans back against the radiator, the darkening sky heavy in the window above his head. I notice the line of his jaw, the gulping translucence of his neck. He stares around the walls of the room as we talk, even though there's nothing to look at.

Interviewer: But how would you <u>describe</u> it (.) this area

M: Just said (.) fuckin' shithole innit

S: Nah (.) nah (.) come on now (..) it's like (.) bits of it are kind of (...) green

M: GREEN (.) Get you (.) that's like <u>poetry</u> or some shit

Interviewer: There <u>are</u> lots of trees (..) people don't mention that when they talk about this place

S: That's what I'm <u>sayin'</u> (.) they just see a massive estate an' that (.) they see about stabbings or drugs in the paper (.) but most people don't even-

M: They see about that mad cunt downstairs-

Interviewer: Yeah (..) didn't know he was out

C: *(quietly)* Me neither

M: You see about <u>him</u> (.) dragging-

S: LEAVE it now-

M: Not even doing proper time for it (..) ONE year an' then getting tagged up an THAT'S IT-

C: Shut the FUCK up now

M: Sorry mate (…) forgot it was (..) yeah (.) not the best neighbours but (…) you've still got a nice place here Ste

       I've been intruding too much. Letting my own thoughts push through. No-one wants to bring up the subject of Connor's sister and all the horrible shit that happened there, but it's hard not to question it in my own head. Why she would get involved with someone like Naylor. How bad things would have to be for her to turn to *him* of all people. How bad things must have got when she tried to leave. How do I explain these kinds of things when I write up the essay? Is this what Mrs Muldowney means when she talks about contextual factors? Also, I'm worrying about the word 'cunt' and about how I can get Mikey to open another *Hooch* without having to ask for it out loud. Connor's stood up now, with his back to the rest of us and Stephen's gazing down into the tape recorder as if he's chatting it up. He points at the telly, the lamp in the corner, the leatherette sofa with a dreamy kind of smile.

S: So I've got me own place now(.) me own gaff (.) as you can see (..) happy days

M: Better than' sleeping on the <u>streets</u> like-

C: FUCK's sake (.) you didn't (.) you weren't even-

M: YEAH (.) YEAH (.) Back last year before I got banged up-

C: *(sighs)* Don't start

S: Yeah don't start on that-

M: I swear down (.) I was on the street yeah (.) for like a couple of nights (..) down by them big towers called (…)

what they <u>called</u> now

Interviewer: Osprey? Falcon?

M: Birds innit (.) that's what I used to say (…) I'd get me head down each night and look up at the stars an that-

S: Who's the fuckin' poet NOW-

M: And I'd look up at the stars and the Falcon tower (.) an the (..) other one (…) an I'd be like (…) two birds and a sky TV (…) could be worse mate (..) could be fuckin' worse

S: You'd be lucky *(laughs into his beer)*

M: <u>Shut</u> up Ste

The first time Mum met Stephen I thought she'd go mad because I was hanging out with some guy who was seven years older. But he put the charm on and after he left, she said:

"He's a lovely lad, Jade. A lovely lad. And he makes a *cracking* brew."

"He's just a friend, Mum."

"Well you could do worse than someone from round here," she said, looking into the distance with that expression she pulls when she's trying to look weathered and wise. "A lot worse. You remember that next year when you're meeting all those toffs from down south."

Through the window behind Connor's head, I see dying leaves lit by streetlight. They move without rhythm or pattern; they move with the knowledge of something coming to an end. They don't care about Stephen's trance music, the painful optimism in the spread of his arms, his best *Ben Sher-*

man shirt. I turn back to the tape.

Interviewer: So that's what I was going to ask next (…) where do you see yourselves in ten years

S: Still round 'ere (.) definite

M: Yeah same (.) few more scars to show for it like

C: Maybe dead

M: Well yeah (.) if you're gonna join the fuckin' ARMY like (.) yeah (.) what d'you <u>expect</u>

C: Maybe dead (.) maybe not (..) might of made Captain

M: Nah (.) it's Lieutenant mate (.) Second Lieutenant THEN Lieutenant THEN Captain

C: I fuckin' KNOW that (.) but you know (…) in ten years (.) I won't be here

(Bangs from downstairs)

Interviewer: What do you mean (.) you won't be here

C: I mean I won't be <u>round</u> here

M: Thought you meant dead again *(laughs)* stop talkin' about bein' fuckin' <u>dead</u>

But Connor does have that look about him. The type of face they use for adverts when they recruit. The kind of life that is loaded and shot out all over places that have got nothing to do with him. He is too quiet, too passive. Passionate only about the subjects he wants to avoid. He stands at the window, scanning the street below as the leaves fall. Stephen's favourite song has come on again, all rolling keys and rapturous female vocals waiting for the beat to drop.

He's closing his eyes and singing along but quiet, so no-one can hear. Mikey's finished rolling now, twisting the ends of Rizla into a fine point. Then Connor leans closer to the glass, looking down. His voice tightens.

C: Turn the tunes off

M: Alright (.) alright (.) don't be a mard (..) what was the question again

Interviewer: Ten years (.) where will you be

S: *(coughs)* I don't see myself movin' or nothin' but sometimes I think I wanna be here but different-

C: Turn the tunes off

S: Different like (.) havin kids an that-

M: Everyone's got fuckin' kids round here (.) his SISTER *(nods at Connor)* his SISTER'S got one off-

C: Turn them OFF NOW

(More bangs from below, getting louder. Mikey turns the music off.)

S: I don't mean like that (.) I mean doin' it proper like

Interviewer: I know (.) I get it

(The banging stops. Silence.)

C: Ste (...) Ste get over 'ere

S: Alright (..) alright

(Stephen crosses to the window)

C: Can you see him (.) can you see him Ste

S: Nah mate (..) the tag (.) how far can he go with the tag on

(Loud crash against the door)

C: Oh <u>SHIT</u> (.) I fuckin <u>TOLD</u> YOU

S: Fuck (.) FUCK (.) we need to-

M: *(standing)* I don't CARE me (.) I'll fuckin' ANSWER it (.) I'll fuckin' answer ANYONE

Interviewer: I don't think you should (.) Mikey (.) MIKEY

S: *(to Connor)* did you see (.) he had a fuckin' (.) a fuckin'-

A hammer. He has a fucking hammer. At five minutes and twenty-five seconds into the tape, there is the sound of Mikey opening the door and then the sound of Darren Naylor making one lunging smash into the electric meter and a second into Mikey's face.

The lights blink on-off until darkness catches up with what's happening. What *is* happening? The heft of metal against flesh, against tooth, against bone. I'm in the hallway looking down, my eyes adjusting to the thick, buzzing shadows. I see Mikey's hands fly to his mouth and Naylor slowly raising his head to look up. His hands are tight round the hammer, about to swing again. Stephen and Connor push past me and stagger down the stairs towards Mikey who lurches forwards to ram his shoulder against the door. Connor throws the bulk of his body against it too and Stephen yanks the bolt across. I can smell how scared we all are. I can hear it, in the scrabbling panic of our bodies. The bannister is slippery under my palm. Mikey turns and starts to climb past the others, towards me. He stumbles and spits into his hands. Looks down at the three broken teeth that have been knocked out of his head.

"It's alright," he keeps trying to say, the blood bubbling from his mouth. "It's alright." I go back into the living room and switch off the tape.

While the events transcribed may be thought of as dramatic or surprising, from a linguistic perspective the findings are very much in line with established research.

"Get him a towel," says Connor, and Stephen comes back with a grimy-looking dishcloth. Connor shakes his head and disappears into the bathroom, coming back with some wet toilet roll that he presses against the swollen mush of Mikey's lips. I sit there, watching the way he does it. There's something meticulous about it, something practised. We can still hear the crash and roar of Naylor on the street, so Stephen jerks the blind down across the window. But he pulls too hard and it slips, flimsily, to the floor.

As expected in male-to-male interaction, the speakers compete for dominance using a combination of raised volume, interruption and expletive. We also see many examples of face-threatening behaviour where participants insult one another or undermine the self-image a speaker is trying to project.

Connor steps back and looks down at the dark clumps of toilet roll in his hand. Stephen finds a candle from under the sink. Mikey lights his joint with shaking hands.

"Reckon I'll get any dosh?" he asks, after a while.

We all look at him. His shape is monstrous in the candle-light and his words are soft as pulp.

"Who off?" Stephen says, and Mikey laughs.

"Off the fuckin' tooth fairy!" He throws his head back, opening that terrible mouth.

Of interest is the extent to which participants follow the conversational cues set by the interviewer. Mikey's utterances often diverge from the questions asked, using covert prestige forms and

*making irrelevant topic shifts so he can tell jokes and draw attention
to his own experiences.*

The carpet is littered with cig-ends and cans and
eventually Mikey slides onto it, his bruised lips open and
snoring. The flat smells ripe with cannabis and sweat. The
swivel ashtray has stopped working, or at least we have
stopped using it. No-one wants to go home in case Naylor's
still stalking about down there, so Stephen tells us we can
sleep over. He looks at the floor as he says it. The dark behind
his head is cavernous as if Naylor has smashed all Stephen's
dreams from the air. He picks up the empty tins and bottles
and I hear them clanking down into a bin in the tiny kitchen.
He comes back and blows out the candle, smooths down his
shirt. He looks at me in the slant of streetlight from the window. Then he looks at Connor.

"Night then," he says.

*Stephen is demonstrably more cooperative than the other
participants in that he responds appropriately to the topics introduced
and attempts to use a level of formality similar to that of the interviewer.*

"Night," I say. But he has gone.

The card he gave me was pink with flowers and heavy
with the weight of something that'd been thought about for
far too long. 'To a Special Friend' it said in gold letters on
the front. It didn't stop him from spelling the word 'special'
wrong on the inside. Or the word 'intelligent'. And the
thought of him getting into bed alone on the other side of the
wall doesn't stop me from reaching out to the body that is
already searching for mine in the dark.

We don't do much. Just enough for me to feel the
heat of him. The anger under his quietness. Just enough for

him to unzip and trace the parts of me that are neither intelligent nor special. Just a body with its own low and simple buzz of pleasure.

Although Connor is noticeably less engaged in the interview, his speech habits provide a great deal of supporting evidence for linguistic theories about gender and social class. He regularly uses imperatives, interrupts frequently and often responds to questions with short, monosyllabic utterances.

I know Connor isn't bothered about me as a person, and that makes it better. I know he's thinking about Naylor downstairs, about his sister being dragged by her hair into the back of that car last year. A memory of her flashes through my head as he touches me; a girl from the year above wearing platform shoes and a high pony. He presses himself into me. I know he is thinking about how he wasn't fast enough when he heard the banging at the door. How he stood back and let Mikey deal with it. How animals like Naylor will smash and smash into people who are already broken.

After a while, we stop. We lie together, hot and fearful. A shaft of sunlight will pour and melt across a room as time passes, but a slice of streetlight stays where it is. The same infected orange colour, the same angle, unmoving, sleepless.

There is a general sense that the speakers will not try to leave the area they describe as a 'shithole' but, for the most part, this does not seem to cause sadness or pain.

When I get up in the morning, Connor pretends to be flat out. Mikey is rolled over, face against sofa, breathing heavily. In the next room I hear Stephen yawning theatrically to warn us he's awake. I pack the tape recorder back into my bag. I want to speak to them, without speaking. To throw

23

light on parts of the night that were good. It had been fun, in a way, hadn't it? So, before I go, I leave three pounds on the table next to Mikey's teeth.

I know it's wrong as soon as the door closes behind me. I know, as I walk home in the morning drizzle, that I won't see Stephen again. They won't want to talk about me and how I sucked up their lives into a spool of dark ribbon. Into a cassette with a label marked 'coursework.' "Top girl," they'll say, if I'm ever mentioned. "She'll go far, her." But the mood will be shifty, and my three-pound joke will roll across the table, falling forever flat.

Mrs Muldowney will get her essay and I will get into Durham. But I will lose this place and its sounds too. They will become alien to me. The muscle and mouth of them. Their volume and capacity. Their ability to convey anger, desire, despair. The fucking flair of it all. I feel it fading away as I trudge up Shadow Brook Road through soggy leaves, breathing in the smell of their rotting.

It is perhaps note-worthy that Stephen's language contradicts expectations when he talks about his hopes of meeting someone and having children in a way that is 'proper'. Research would suggest that this kind of self-disclosure is particularly rare in men from this socioeconomic class. The willingness to make himself vulnerable to ridicule for the sake of participating fully and honestly proves to be an admirable exception to the 'rules', and perhaps reminds us of the limitations of applying academic theory to the lives of individuals.

He will be making the first brew of the day now, picking up the cig-ends from the floor. Connor will help, without meeting his eyes. And Mikey will be waking, running tongue over gums, to a sore and fresh sense of loss.

Mrs Muldowney is nearing the end. On the final page, surely. There have been one or two frowns and a few tilts of the head. There was the moment when the pointed toe of her shoe started to kick slightly at the leg of the desk. But then she shook her head, cleared her throat, and reduced herself back to blankness.

I hear bodies outside on the corridor waiting for their next lesson, see them leaning against the little window of the classroom door. The wind shakes the trees outside and stubby fingers tap the glass. Mrs Muldowney puts the last sheet of paper down and raises an eyebrow.

"My goodness, Jade. What a rich and varied life you lead."

I say nothing.

"The essay should get an A with a few tweaks." She announces it coolly, without praise. She looks at the paper again, then back at me. "But I have to warn you to be more careful about... who you choose to spend time with outside of college." The tip of her shoe has started to nudge the desk again. I feel it like a prod in the chest. "Going to flats like this with men like..."- she flicks back to the introductory paragraph of the essay and taps a sharp fingernail against the page- "men like Stephen? Mikey? Can it really be *safe?*" The question hangs in the air as if it has answered itself.

I stare past her head at the sugar paper display. My arms are tightly folded, fingers digging into the muscle that exists, somewhere, under my coat. If I squeeze hard enough, I can stop the words from flickering about in my mouth. I can stop the anger from lurching around, grasping at injustices, smashing things up.

Author Biography

Louise Finnigan lives and writes in Manchester. Her work has been longlisted for The Mairtin Crawford Award and shortlisted for The Cambridge Short Story Prize. Last year, she was a finalist in The Manchester Fiction Prize. Her work has appeared, and is due to appear, in various anthologies and she has been published online with Storgy. Louise is interested in writing from the perspectives of working-class teenagers who are negotiating their identity in a world which requires them to change themselves if they are to 'escape'. Her stories are set on council estates, in high-rise flats and failing schools and aim to present the complexity of situations which might be easily dismissed as non-literary. All settings are Mancunian or linked to the city in some way, and all characters are drawn with love.

Enjoy the rest of our 2021 Shorts Season:

Pigskin by David Hartley

Something strange is happening to the animals on the farm. A pig becomes bacon, chickens grow breadcrumbs, a cow turns to leather, a goat excretes cheese. As food becomes scarce and the looming 'pot-bellies' threaten to invade the safety of the sty, Pig knows he must get to the bottom of this strange phenomenon or face imminent death. Reminiscent of Animal Farm and darkly satirical, David Hartley interrogates the ethics of farming and the potential problems of genetic engineering, asking important questions about our relationship to the food – or animals – we eat.

"Pigskin is a knife-sharp, knowing fable about animal instincts and human ingenuity. David Hartley has a gift for creating stories that leave scars."

- Aliya Whiteley, author of The Loosening Skin

PowerPoint Eulogy by Mark Wilson

Three corporate hours have been allotted to commemorate the life of enigma, Bill Motluck. Employee memories of his life are crudely recounted onto a dusty projector. No one has ever been quite sure of his purpose. No one is quite sure who wrote the PowerPoint...but it seems to be exposing them all, one by one.

"In his wildly imaginative chapbook, PowerPoint Eulogy, Chicago writer and visual artist Mark Wilson paints a picture of corporate culture—and humanity at large—that is both soul-crushingly bleak and hilariously demented. Divided into forty-four presenta-tion "slides", the story centers on the memories a group of unnamed employees have of their recently deceased co-worker, Bill Motluck—a man so bland he enjoyed small talk about skim milk, and so desper-ate to fit in he once rented a newborn for Bring Your Kid to Work

Day. Should we give in to the impulse to laugh at poor Bill, or feel sympathy for his plight? As the stories and little revelations pile up, it becomes harder and harder to decide—and the tension this creates is what ultimately makes this one-of-a-kind collection so impossible to put down. I laughed, I winced, I loved it".

- Mark Rader, Author of 'The Wanting Life'.

Hassan's Zoo by Ruth Brandt

Hassan's Zoo

When American soldiers invade Iraq searching for weapons of mass destruction, Kesari the Bengal tiger and other wildlife are at the mercy of guns and keeper, Hassan.

Entrenched in perpetual fear, Hassan must exercise Godly powers over his creatures in his attempts to save them - and himself.

A Village in Winter

"Mrs Gregory said to leave Frizz and his mum be for a while. Stop pestering. That poor woman with that lad."

In the chill of winter, the villagers play by the river, their play as harsh as the ice.

How To Bring Him Back by Claire HM

'If I was going to cast a spell tonight, this night of a full arse moon as stark and crunchy as a ten-day crust of snow, I'd start by telling the earth to spin in the opposite direction.

By what power?

By the power of my pen.'

'How to Bring Him Back' is a journey into a darkly humorous love triangle. It's 90s Birmingham and Cait is post-university, aimless and working in a dive bar. She's caught between Stadd, who's stable, funny, compatible as a friend, and her compulsive sexual attraction with Rik. Present day Cait picks up her pen, on her yearly writing retreat to Ab-

erystwyth, and addresses an absent Stadd with the lessons she
has learnt from her past.

Exploring the dynamics of desire and consent while reflecting
upon the damage people can inflict on each other in
relationships, Claire is an exciting and bold writer for the
modern age.

The Guts of a Mackerel by Clare Reddaway

*"Who's Bobby Sands?" she asked, as she laid the fish on the face of
a smiling young man with long wavy hair. "And what's a hunger
strike?"*

On a family holiday to her dad's Irish homeland, Eve's
concerns about impressing local boy Liam are confronted by
the stark reality of political and personal divisions during the
Troubles. Former friends have turned into enemies, and this
country of childhood memory is suddenly a lot less
welcoming.

About Fly on the Wall Press

A publisher with a conscience.
Publishing high quality anthologies on pressing issues, chapbooks and poetry products, from exceptional poets around the globe.
Founded in 2018 by founding editor, Isabelle Kenyon.

Other publications:

Please Hear What I'm Not Saying (February 2018. Anthology, profits to Mind.)

Persona Non Grata (October 2018. Anthology, profits to Shelter and Crisis Aid UK.)

Bad Mommy / Stay Mommy by Elisabeth Horan (May 2019. Chapbook.)

The Woman With An Owl Tattoo by Anne Walsh Donnelly (May 2019. Chapbook.)

the sea refuses no river by Bethany Rivers (June 2019. Chapbook.)

White Light White Peak by Simon Corble (July 2019. Artist's Book.)

Second Life by Karl Tearney (July 2019. Full collection)

The Dogs of Humanity by Colin Dardis (August 2019. Chapbook.)

Small Press Publishing: The Dos and Don'ts by Isabelle Kenyon (January 2020. Non-Fiction.)

Alcoholic Betty by Elisabeth Horan (February 2020. Chapbook.)

Awakening by Sam Love (March 2020. Chapbook.)

Grenade Genie by Tom McColl (April 2020. Full Collection.)

House of Weeds by Amy Kean and Jack Wallington
(May 2020. Full Collection.)
No Home In This World by Kevin Crowe
(June 2020. Short Stories.)
How To Make Curry Goat by Louise McStravick
(July 2020. Full Collection.)
The Goddess of Macau by Graeme Hall
(August 2020. Short Stories.)
The Prettyboys of Gangster Town by Martin Grey
(September 2020. Chapbook.)
The Sound of the Earth Singing to Herself by Ricky Ray
(October 2020. Chapbook.)
Mancunian Ways (Anthology of poetry and photography)
Inherent by Lucia Orellana Damacela
(November 2020. Chapbook.)
Medusa Retold by Sarah Wallis
(December 2020. Chapbook.)
We Are All Somebody compiled by Samantha Richards (February
2021. Anthology. Profits to Street Child United.)
Pigskin by David Hartley
(February 2021. Shorts.)
Aftereffects by Jiye Lee
(March 2021. Chapbook.)
Someone Is Missing Me by Tina Tamsho-Thomas
(March 2021. Full Collection.)
PowerPoint Eulogy by Mark Wilson
(April 2021. Shorts)

Social Media:
@fly_press (Twitter)
@flyonthewall_poetry (Instagram)
@flyonthewallpress (Facebook)